Choose Your Own Journey

Written by Susie Brooks

Illustrated by Tracy Cottingham

Kane Miller
A DIVISION OF EDC PUBLISHING

Come on, everyone, let's go!

Choose the **BOAT**, the **TRAIN**, the **CAR** or the **BIKE** and follow each adventure with your finger.

See where the journey takes you –
then pick another vehicle and try again!

Some sleepy people are still in their beds,
but we're all on the move!

The train **CLICKETY-CLACKS** along its
tracks, while the boat swooshes forward
with a **BOOM** from its horn.

BRRRRM goes the car as it passes the park.
Can it catch up with the **whirly-wheeled** bike?

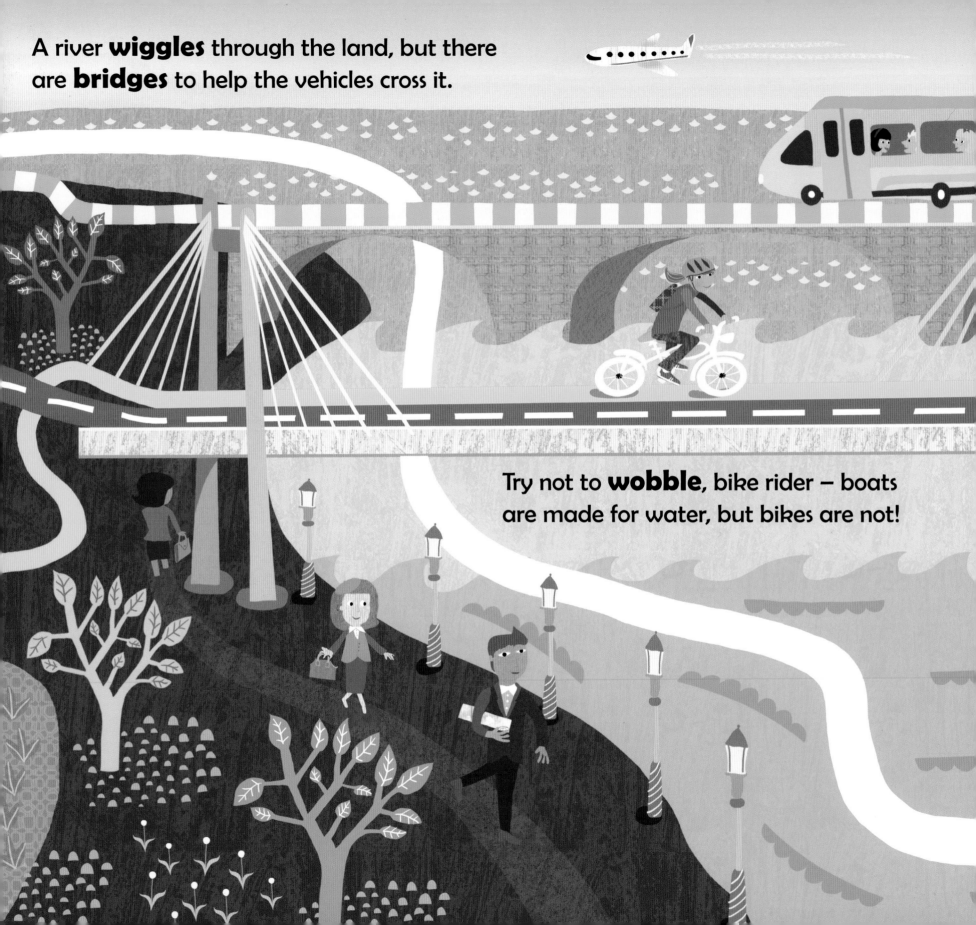

A river **wiggles** through the land, but there are **bridges** to help the vehicles cross it.

Try not to **wobble**, bike rider — boats are made for water, but bikes are not!

The path begins to slope uphill – bike rider,
you'll need some extra **puff**. The car overtakes
and **cruises** ahead. Be careful steering around the bends!

Cutting through a tunnel saves the train a climb.
Switch on the headlights, car driver!
CLICKETY-CLACK, CLICKETY-CLACK . . .

The tractor **trundles** really slowly through the farm — bad luck, car! Will the boat overtake?

On the way to the beach, the sun is **shining bright**. It's cool inside the car, but the bike rider is ready for ice cream.

The captain of the boat **drops anchor** at the jetty. Boat travelers, your journey is over!

Can you hear tummies **rumbling** in the car? It must be time for lunch! The car needs fuel and so do the passengers . . .

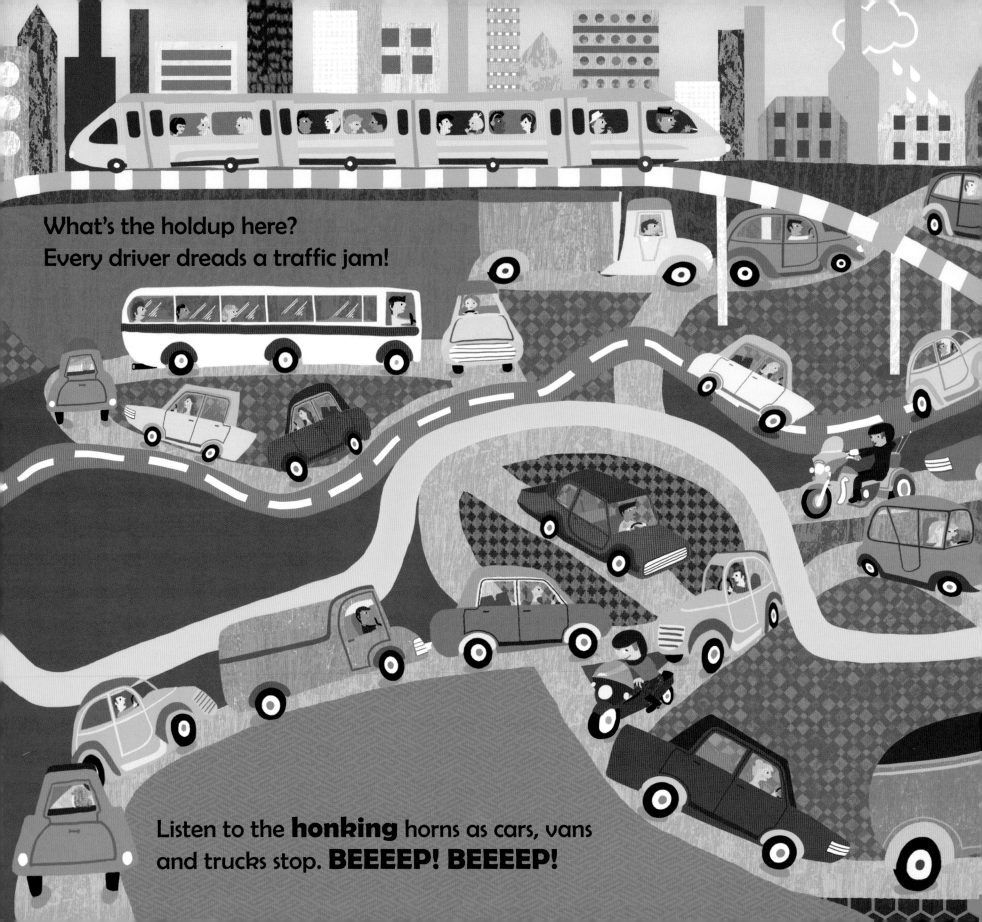

What's the holdup here?
Every driver dreads a traffic jam!

Listen to the **honking** horns as cars, vans
and trucks stop. **BEEEEP! BEEEEP!**

Good news for the train and
the bike – your routes are clear!

At last, the car can move again — but the train is pulling into a station. The signal goes red and the **brakes go on**. Time to get off, train travelers!

Bike rider, put your coat on quickly or you'll get wet!

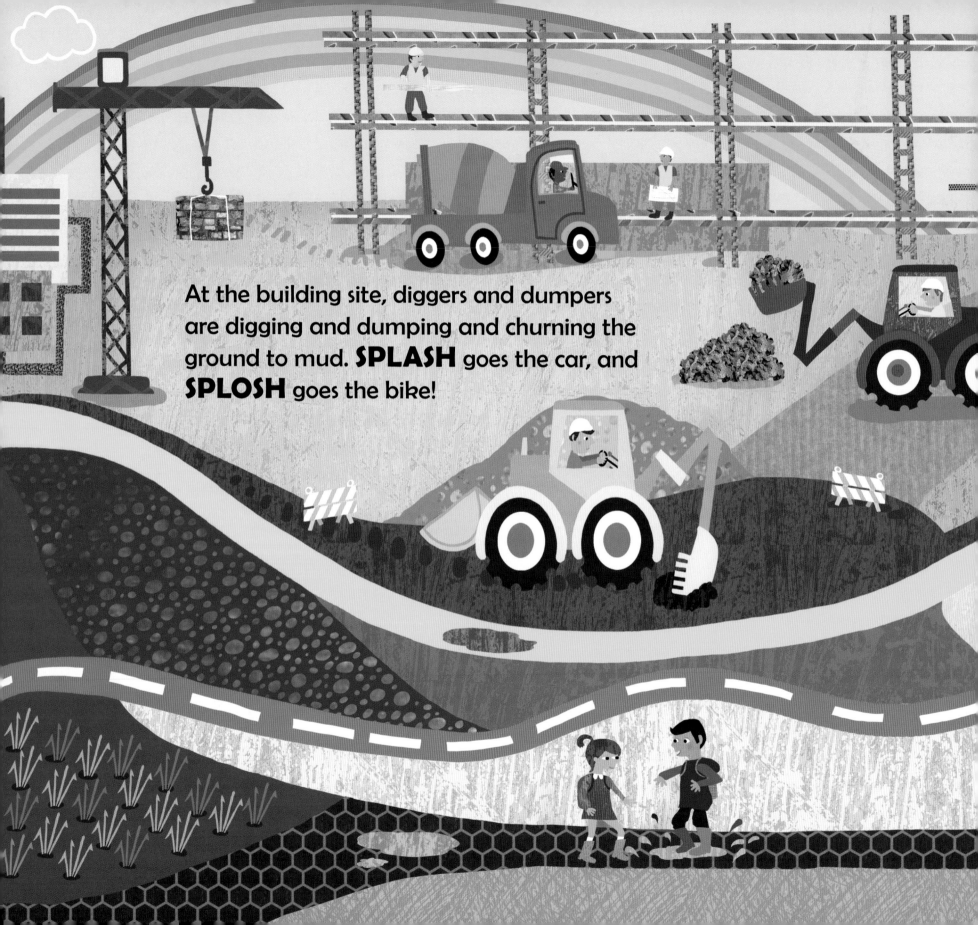

At the building site, diggers and dumpers are digging and dumping and churning the ground to mud. **SPLASH** goes the car, and **SPLOSH** goes the bike!

A nail pops a tire –
bike rider, you need to stop
and fix that flat.

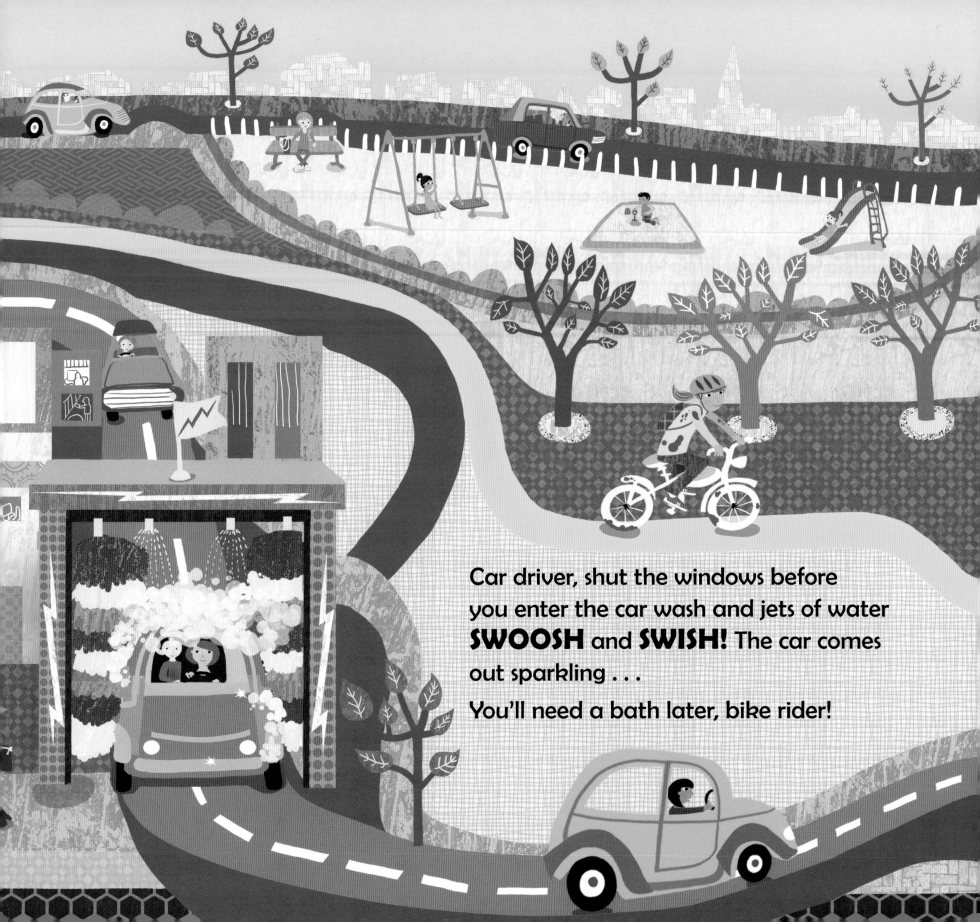

Car driver, shut the windows before you enter the car wash and jets of water **SWOOSH** and **SWISH!** The car comes out sparkling . . .

You'll need a bath later, bike rider!

Tummies are **rumbling** in the car again –
it's time to stop for pizza!

Bike rider, where are you off to?

The carnival is full of fast and exciting rides. Watch the Ferris wheel whirl and the ghost train **WHOOO!**

There goes a unicycle – imagine balancing with just one wheel!

It's the end of the day and you're almost home. Bike rider, you must be feeling tired after all that pedaling. **Time for a bath and a good night's sleep!**